D0786478

Rain

In memory of my dad, Lyuba, with whom I enjoyed watching thunderstorms.

Published by Dragonfly Books
an imprint of Random House Children's Books
a division of Random House, Inc., New York

Copyright © 2000 by Manya Stojic
Originally published in hardcover in the United Kingdom by David Bennett Books Limited in 2000.
Published in hardcover by Crown Publishers, an imprint of Random House Children's Books, in 2000.
This edition published by arrangement with Crown Publishers.

All rights reserved. No part of this book may be reproduced or transmitted in any form or by any means, electronic or mechanical, including photocopying, recording, or by any information storage and retrieval system, without the written permission of the publisher, except where permitted by law.
For information address Crown Books for Young Readers.

Dragonfly Books and colophon are registered trademarks of Random House, Inc.

Visit us on the Web! www.randomhouse.com/kids
Educators and librarians, for a variety of teaching tools, visit us at www.randomhouse.com/teachers

The Library of Congress has cataloged the hardcover edition of this work as follows:
Stojic, Manya.
Rain / written and illustrated by Manya Stojic.
p. cm.
Summary: The animals of the African savanna use their senses to predict and then enjoy the rain.
ISBN: 978-0-517-80085-0 (trade)—ISBN: 978-0-517-80086-7 (lib. bdg.)
[1. Rain and rainfall—Fiction. 2. Zoology—Africa—Fiction.
3. Senses and sensation—Fiction. 4. Africa—Fiction.] I. Title.
PZ7.S873Rai 2000
[E]—dc21 99035298

ISBN: 978-0-385-73729-6 (pbk.)
Reprinted by arrangement with Crown Books for Young Readers
MANUFACTURED IN CHINA
First Dragonfly Books Edition
April 2009
10 9 8 7 6 5 4 3 2 1

Random House Children's Books supports the First Amendment and celebrates the right to read.

Rain

WRITTEN AND ILLUSTRATED BY

MANYA STOJIC

Dragonfly Books New York

It was hot.
Everything was hot and dry.

The red soil was hot and dry
and cracked.

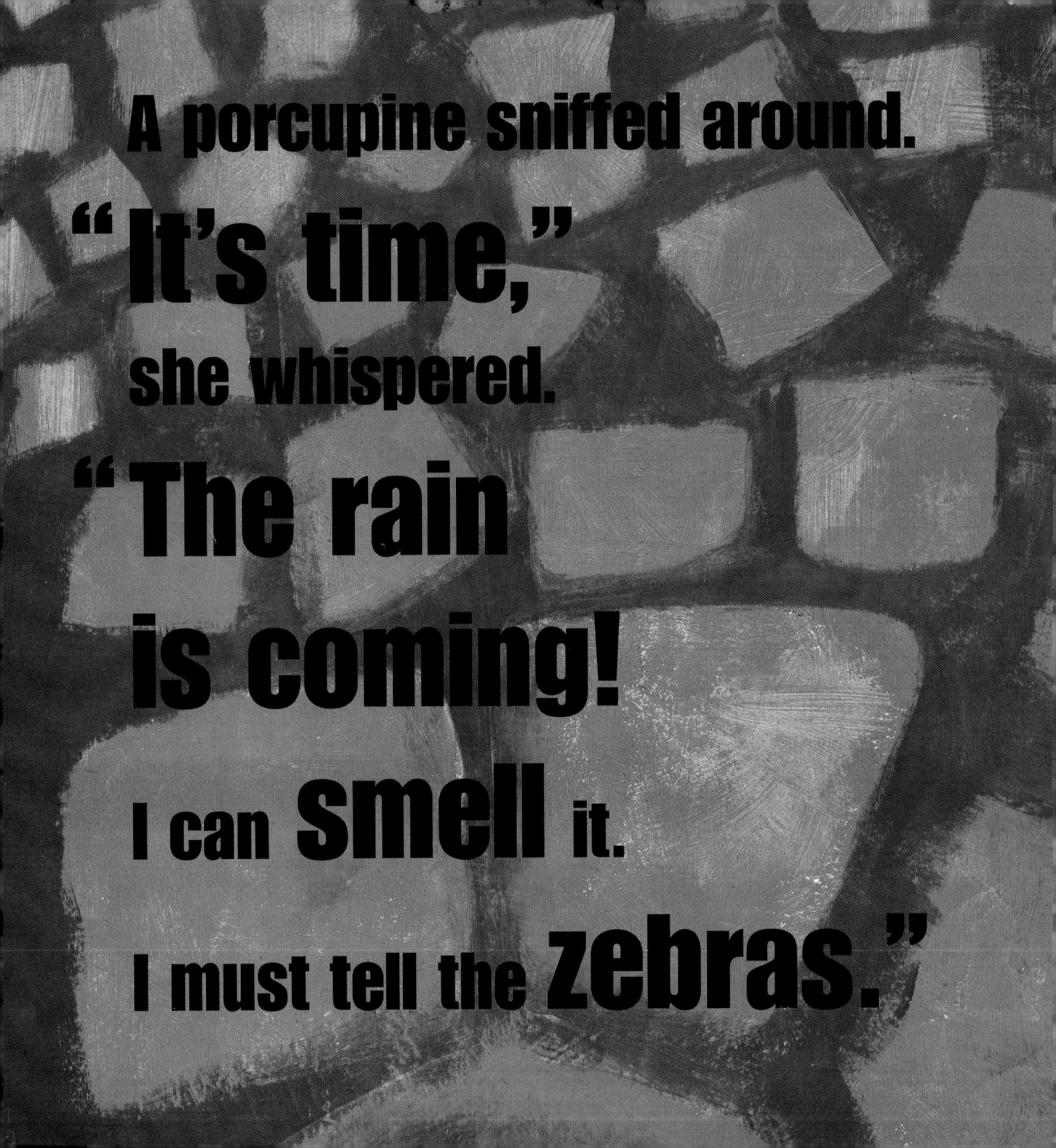

A porcupine sniffed around.

"It's time,"

she whispered.

"The rain

is coming!

I can smell it.

I must tell the zebras."

Lightning flashed.
"The rain is coming!"
said the zebras.

"Porcupine can smell it.
We can see it. We must
tell the baboons."

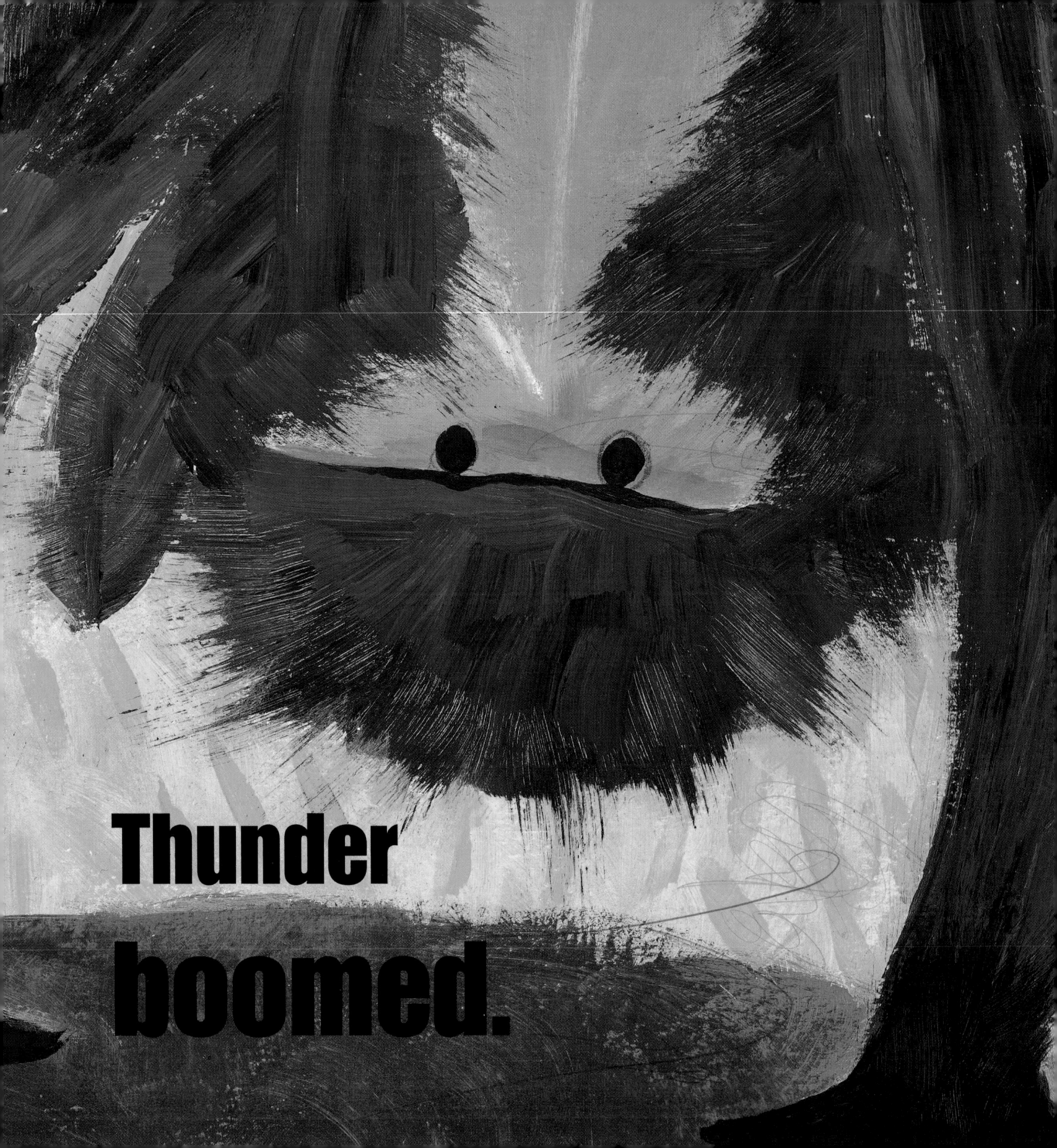
Thunder
boomed.

"The rain is coming!"
cried the baboons.

"Porcupine
can smell it.
The zebras
can see it.
We can **hear** it.
We must tell
the **rhino.**"

A raindrop **splashed.**

"The rain is here!"

said the rhino.

"Porcupine smelled it.

The zebras saw it.

The baboons heard it.

And I felt it.
I must tell
the lion."

The lion spoke in a deep **purr.**

"Yes, the rain is here.

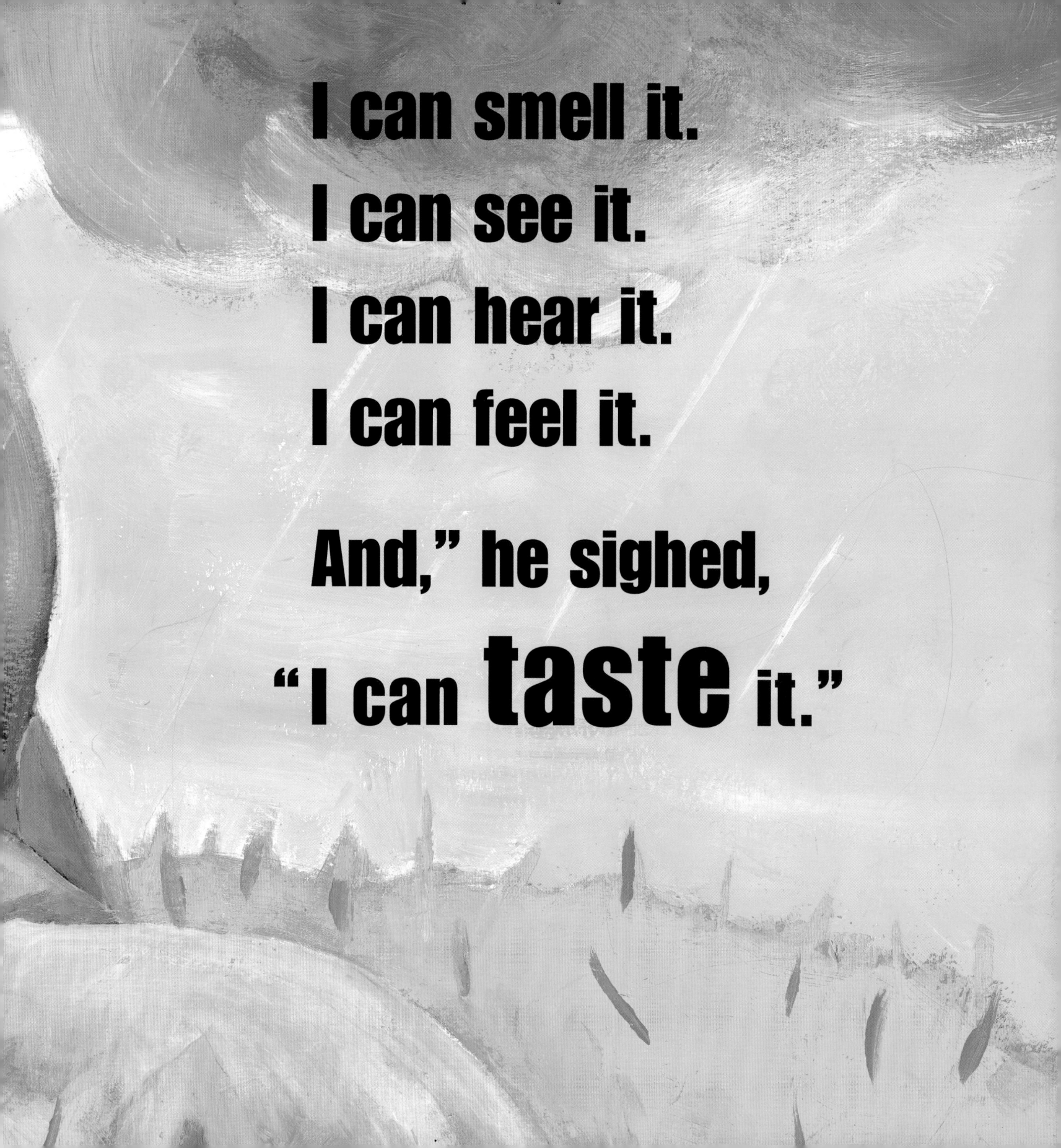

I can smell it.
I can see it.
I can hear it.
I can feel it.

And," he sighed,
"I can **taste** it."

It rained
and it
rained
and it
rained.

It rained until every river
gushed and gurgled.
It rained until every water hole
was full.

Then the rain stopped and everywhere long, feathery grasses grew from the soil.

Every tree began to sprout fresh, green leaves.

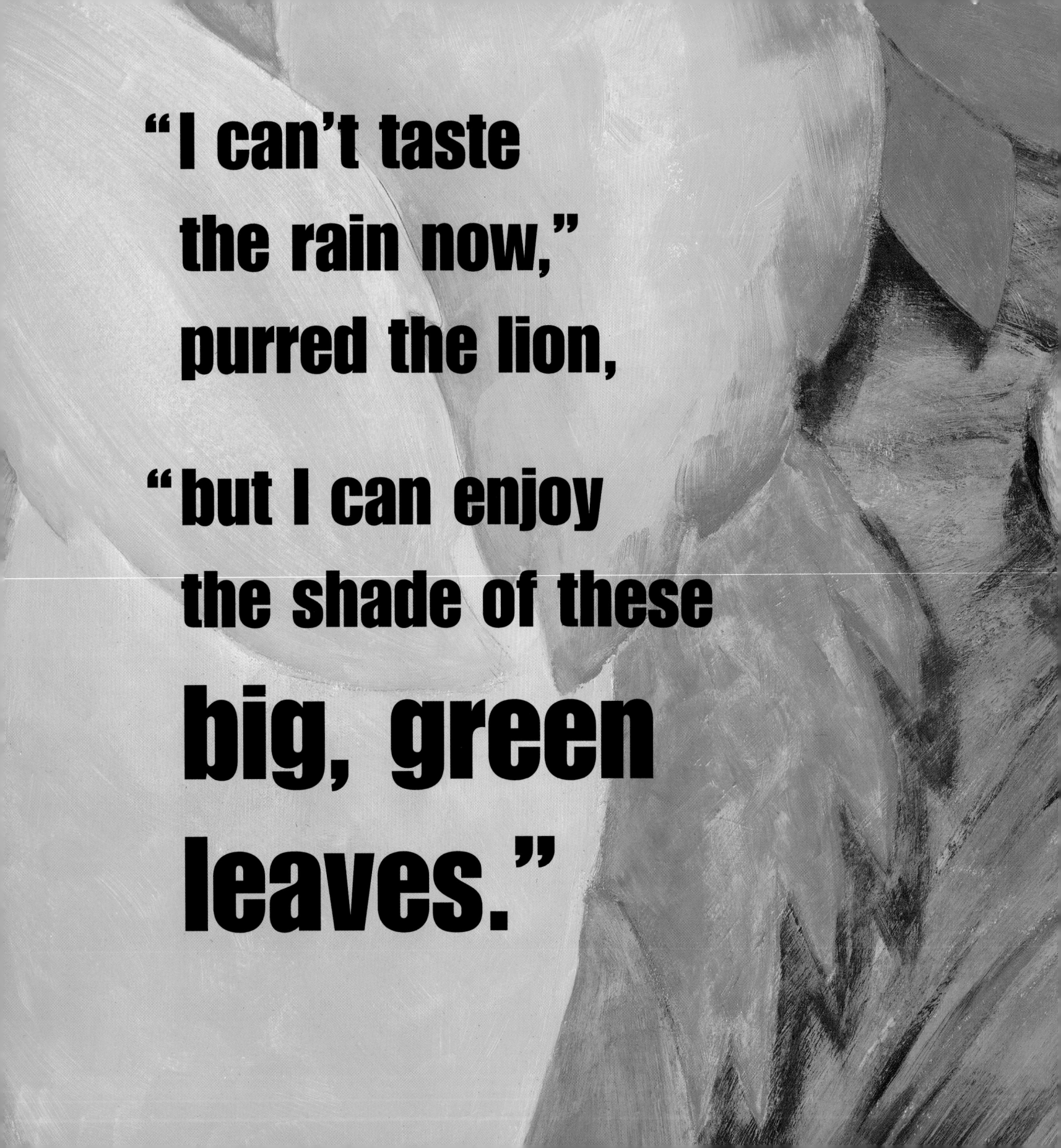

"I can't taste the rain now," purred the lion,

"but I can enjoy the shade of these big, green leaves."

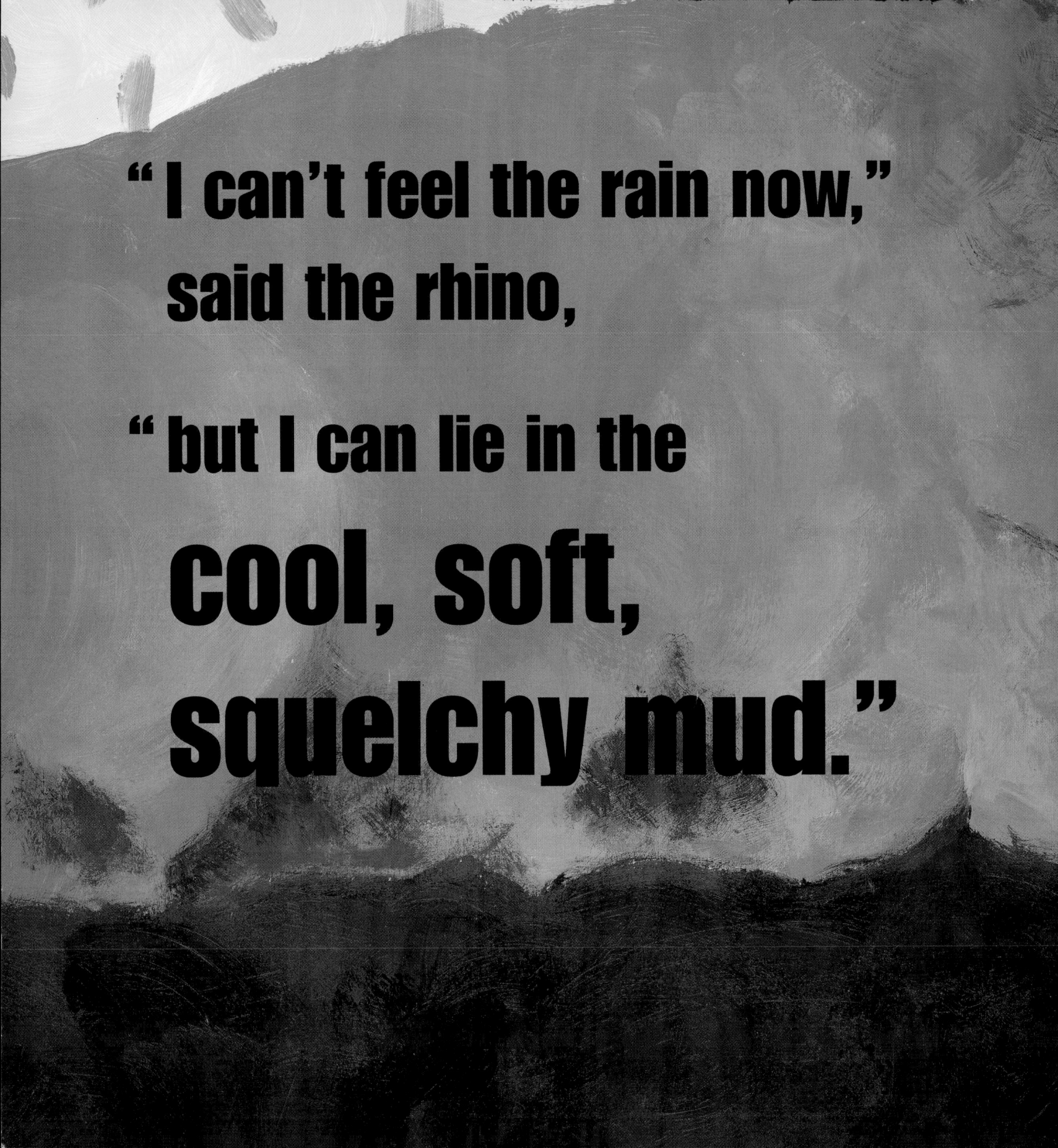
"I can't feel the rain now,"
said the rhino,
"but I can lie in the
cool, soft,
squelchy mud."

"We can't hear the rain now,"
shouted the baboons,

"but we can eat
fresh,
juicy fruit
from the trees."

"We can't see the rain now," said the zebras, "but we can have a **refreshing drink** from the water hole."

"I can't smell the rain now,"
whispered the porcupine,
"but I know that it will
come back again.
When it's
time."

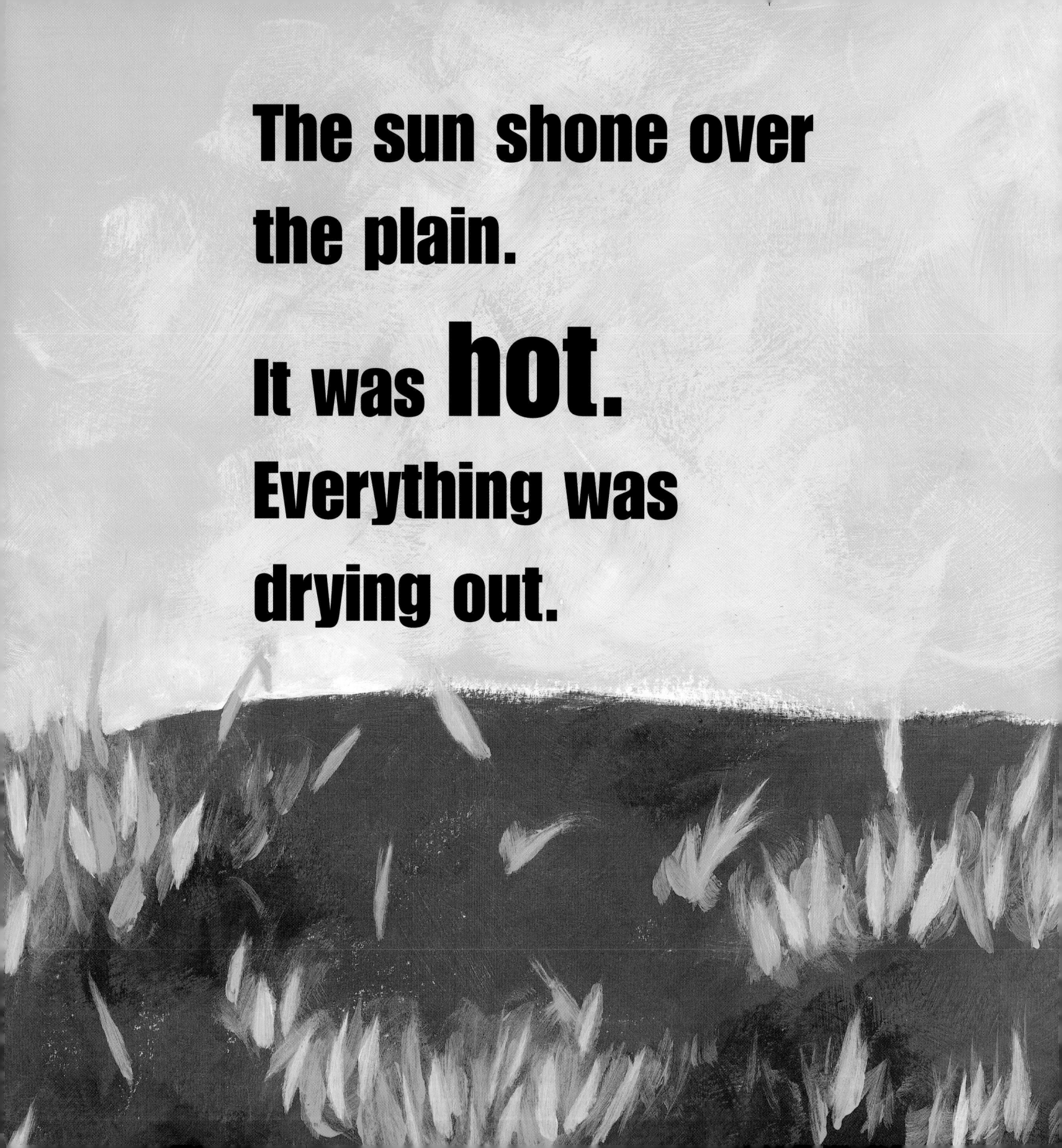

The sun shone over the plain.

It was **hot.** Everything was drying out.

The red soil was hot and dry.
A tiny crack appeared.